USBORNE SIMPLE REA

THE MAMMOTH HUNT

Heather Amery
Illustrated by Colin King

Language Consultant: Betty Root
Reading and Language Information Centre
University of Reading, England

This family lived thousands and thousands of years ago. They lived in a big, dark cave.

This is Ruff and Hazel.   This is Dad and Mum.

This is Uncle Birch, little Fern, Aunt Holly, Granny and baby Moss.

3

It is very early in the morning. Everyone is
having breakfast.

Dad and Uncle Birch are going to hunt a
huge mammoth. After breakfast they get ready.

Hazel holds Dad's spear.
It has a stone blade.

Ruff helps to tie up
Uncle Birch's boots.

Dad and Uncle Birch go off to meet their friends.
Ruff and Hazel have to stay in the cave.

Baby Fern falls over and starts to cry. Mum turns round to pick her up.

Hazel and Ruff tiptoe out of the cave. No one sees them go.

6

They follow the hunters along the river bank.
Sometimes they have to hide behind the rocks.

Hazel sees a fish in
the water.

Ruff tries to hit it with
his spear.

The hunters are nearly at the top of the hill.
Hazel and Ruff run after them.

Suddenly they see a wolf on the path. It walks
slowly towards them.

8

Ruff shouts and throws his spear at the wolf.
Hazel throws some stones at it.

The wolf snarls at them
but walks away.

Hazel and Ruff run on
up the hill.

At the top, they stop and stare. There is a
huge mammoth eating grass and weeds.
10

The hunters shout and run towards it.
Uncle Birch is in front with his new sharp spear.

Ruff and Hazel run
towards the hunters.

They hide behind a rock
to watch them.

The mammoth sees the hunters. It lifts its
great head and roars. Then it charges.

Brave Uncle Birch stabs it with his spear.

The mammoth hits him with its tusks.

Uncle Birch falls down. He is hurt.
The hunters try to kill the mammoth.

Hazel and Ruff run to help Uncle Birch.
They are afraid the mammoth will tread on him.

Uncle Birch groans and tries to sit up.
His arm hurts but he is not bleeding.

14

Ruff helps him to stand up. The mammoth roars.
It is charging straight at Hazel.

15

She runs away as fast as she can.

But she slips on a wet stone and falls down.

The mammoth chases her. It is getting closer. Hazel manages to get up and run on.

She reaches some rocks and starts to climb them.
Ruff is there to pull her up.

The mammoth stops. It is stuck in the mud.
The hunters kill it with their spears.

Dad picks up Hazel.
Her knee still hurts.

He carries her back to
Uncle Birch.

Uncle Birch is feeling better now.
They all walk back down the path to the cave.

Mum is waiting for them. She has been very worried about Hazel and Ruff.

The hunters come home, carrying meat and the mammoth's tusks. Tonight there will be a feast.

Later, Uncle Birch calls Hazel and Ruff.

He takes them far into the cave. It is very dark.

They walk down a long tunnel in the rock.
Uncle Birch has something special to show them.

Suddenly they come to a huge, high cave.
On the walls are paintings of animals and hunters.

Uncle Birch takes Hazel and Ruff back again.
The feast is nearly ready.

22

Everyone sits round the fire. There is lots to eat.
They all talk about the mammoth hunt.

After the feast, Hazel and Ruff go to bed.
Mum tucks them up under warm furs.

First published in 1987. Usborne Publishing Ltd, 20 Garrick Street, London WC2E 9BJ, England. © Usborne Publishing Ltd, 1987.